WORLD WAR II TALES
TERRY DEARY

THE PHANTOM FARM

Illustrated by James de la Rue

A & C BLACK
AN IMPRINT OF BLOOMSBURY
LONDON   NEW DELHI   NEW YORK   SYDNEY

Chapter 1

Decks and necks

A village near Portsmouth, 1941

Do you believe in ghosts? I did once.
When I was a schoolgirl during the Second
World War.

My dad ran the White Horse Inn,
serving beer and sandwiches to sailors
and farmers as well as the local people.
Mum went out every day to work in the
dockyards of Portsmouth.

'What do you *do* there, Mum?' I asked.

Her eyes went as wide as beer mugs.
'It's secret, Rose. It's so secret I'd be

thrown in jail if I told you. Hitler's spies are everywhere. You know what the posters say?'

'Careless talk costs lives,' I whispered. She wrapped her flowery pinafore round herself and headed for the door. 'Is it dangerous, Mum?'

'Deadly,' she said and hurried off to catch the bus that would take her to the dockyard.

Dad spat in a glass and polished it with a dusty cloth. He sighed. 'She's a cleaner. When the warships come into port she cleans them—washes the bedclothes, dusts the cabins and scrubs the floors and decks.'

'Is that top secret?'

'No, lass, it's just your mum's little joke. See?'

I thought about it. 'Not really.' I had a lot to learn.

I remember the evening I first saw Slick Sam. It was dark outside and we'd drawn the blackout curtains. Dad turned up the gas lamps and lit the log fire. It was cosy in the tap room and the lounge bar. All we needed was a few customers.

The first to step through the door was Jack Latham. Mr Latham was usually the first every night. He wore a grey overcoat and was so tall his head brushed the top of the door. Dad said he was so tall because his neck was twice as long as any normal neck.

'He has a neck like Nat Jackley, the Rubber Man,' Dad used to laugh... but he never called Mr Latham that to his face. Nat Jackley was a comic who went on stage in the Portsmouth theatres. Nat Jackley in the pantomime was so funny I almost wet my pants laughing at him.

And the words of his song at the end were just right.

I picture the scene on a cold winter's night
With the blackout, the bombs and the Blitz.
The world might be tragic, but inside there
was magic
With the audience rolling in fits.

Nat Jackley made me laugh. But I never dared to laugh at Mr Latham. That night he took his seat at the corner of the bar and ordered, 'The usual.'

I ran to grab a bottle of Golden Ale, took the top off and poured it carefully into a glass. 'There you are Mr Latham.'

'Thank you, Rose... though the law says a girl of your age should not be serving drinks.'

I felt his pale eyes drill into me. 'No, Mr Latham,' I muttered. 'Where's your uniform, Mr Latham?' I asked as he took his first sip.

'I only work as a special constable six days a week. Today's my day off.'

I was a bit shocked. I was going to ask him if all the burglars and spies and shoplifters could get away with it that day. But before I could open my mouth to speak my mouth fell open in wonder.

Slick Sam had walked through the door.

Chapter 2

Shoes and steaks

I'd seen soldiers and sailors on parade in their best uniforms of red, blue and green, silver and gold. But Slick Sam was more dazzling than any of them.

His shoes were yellow. Yellow! He wore a suit of an orangey-red colour with yellow checks. The lapels on his jacket almost touched his arms and the trousers were so tight they must have stopped the blood getting to his toes.

Slick Sam's shoulders were padded to make them wide as a No. 24 bus. He could have poked someone's eye out with them in a crowded room.

His tie was green silk and had a picture of a dancing lady painted on it. On his head was a trilby hat, a couple of sizes too small, tilted to the side like a soldier's cap.

When he spoke he sounded like he came from London, but he spoke faster than a machine gun so it was hard to follow. He stuck his head around the door and saw me, Dad and Mr Latham. He winked at me then shuffled across to Dad with a blur of yellow shoes.

'Good evening boss, and how are you this fine but chilly evening? Now you look like a man who knows a bargain when he sees one. Am I right? I say, am I right? And since you're a man who likes a bargain, you've come to the right man.'

He stretched out a skinny hand to shake my dad's, and Dad began to ask, 'What can I get you, sir?'

'It's more a question of what *I* can get for *you*, my old china plate—that means "mate" where I come from. Slick Sam's my name—but you can call me Slick Sam—and selling goods is me game. Now you tell me what you need and I'll get it for you.'

The man looked over his shoulder, sly as our dog about to pinch a cake off the table. He tapped the side of his nose with a skeleton-thin finger. 'No ration coupons needed, of course. No names, no pack-drill, Bob's your uncle and Charlie's your aunt. Know what I mean?'

Dad turned pale and his eye twitched.

He turned his back on Special Constable Latham so the policeman couldn't see him. Dad jerked his thumb at the constable and mouthed the words, 'He's a copper.'

Slick Sam didn't seem to notice. 'Tell you what, squire, as a special opening offer I can sell you the most delicious piece of beef you ever tasted in your life. I could cut a slice off this young lady here and it wouldn't be as tender as the two rump steaks I have for sale.'

Slick Sam reached inside his long jacket and pulled out a packet wrapped in newspaper. He opened it and showed two slices of raw meat.

My dad gave a tiny shake of the head. And suddenly the man with the yellow shoes understood. 'This is my tea,' he said smoothly. 'What I'm saying is I could get you a piece of steak just *like* this,

if you have the right coupons of course, and *if* you paid the correct price. All above board and shipshape, know what I mean?'

He began to slide the yellow shoes towards the door and hid the meat parcel away again. 'I don't blame you for refusing,' he said in a soft whine. 'There's a lot of crooks about. People selling food without ration books. Bang out of order that is. Spivs, we call them villains in London. I'll bid you goodnight, landlord. Take care.'

And he was gone as quickly as he'd arrived.

'Well I never,' Dad said.

Chapter 3
Chicken and cheats

After Mr Latham had left the bar Dad explained to me. 'You can't buy meat without coupons from your ration book. There's not enough food to go around. Everybody gets the same rations so we share it out, fair and square.'

'I know that, Dad,' I said.

He spat in a glass. 'Ah, but it's not that simple, because everybody wants a little bit extra. You've seen Farmer Edwards come in here?'

'Yes, Dad.' I remembered the short, heavy man in cow-smelling clothes.

'Let's say Farmer Edwards has fifty chickens. He tells the ration inspector he has *forty*—they can't go around counting every chicken in the country. That means the farmer has ten spare chickens nobody knows about. See?'

'No, Dad.'

Dad sighed. 'Farmer Edwards brought one of those spare chickens in here last week. We had it for Sunday dinner, remember? And your mum had enough left over to make chicken pie on Monday. Now your mum and me didn't give Farmer Edwards any coupons or any money for that chicken. I gave him four pints of free beer, see?'

I gasped. 'But that's breaking the law, Dad. They'll lock you up. Miss Weardale our teacher says people that do that are wicked. She says it's a black market. She said they're parachutes.'

'I think you mean parasites. Anyway...' Dad lowered his voice. '*Most* people say it makes sense. *You* get fed, the farmer gets a nice drink and no one gets hurt.'

'Except the chicken,' I argued.

Dad rolled his eyes up to the ceiling.

'The chicken never felt a thing. Just remember, everybody cheats a little bit.'

'Even Mr Latham?'

Dad rubbed his bristling chin. It was hard to find new razor blades in the shops. 'Not Mr Latham. He wants to see every ration cheat locked away.'

I was worried. 'Including you, Dad?'

'Including me, and your mum... and you.'

'Me!' I squawked. 'I never stole no chicken.'

Dad gave a grim smile. 'You ate it, Rosie lass, you ate it.'

I suddenly felt sick. It was as if my Sunday dinner was trying to jump back out of my throat.

'That's why you don't want to go saying anything to Special Constable Latham, girl. It's our secret. Careless talk costs lives—and gets our family locked in prison. Right, Rose?'

'Right, Dad.'

I didn't sleep much that night. I

wondered what it would be like sleeping in a prison cell. That's when I decided the real villain wasn't Farmer Edwards or my dad or my mum or me. It was Slick Sam. If he was behind bars we'd all be safe.

And I was the girl to put him there.

Chapter 4
Steaks and sludge

The next afternoon I was running home after school at dusk, down the winding lane past Edwards' Farm gates, when something caught my eye. I'd have sworn I saw a yellow shoe disappear behind the barn at the back of the farmyard.

Only Slick Sam wore shoes like that. Now *you* might wonder what the spiv was doing in Edwards' farmyard. For some reason *I* only wondered what the mud and sludge would do to his shining, sun-bright shoes.

When I reached the corner of the main street I saw Special Constable Latham standing there, rocking on his heels and watching shoppers hurry home with their bags. It seemed that no one wanted to stop and talk to him. Maybe they had secret shopping in those bags that they'd bought without coupons.

He looked like a proper policeman, but instead of a helmet he wore a black tin hat with 'S.C. Police' in white letters.

'Good evening, young Rose,' he said.

'Good evening Constable,' I said and my voice trembled. If he said the word 'chicken' then I would run around like a chicken crying, *Guilty, I ate it and I didn't have a coupon. Guilty! Lock me away!*

But he said, 'Funny bloke. That feller in the yellow shoes. You know, the one in your pub last night.'

'Yeller in the feller shoes? Sick Sam...

I mean Slick Sam? I just seen him,' I babbled as if my lips were not connected to my brain.

'He's up to something,' the constable growled. 'It's just a matter of catching him at it. I reckon he's selling meat off the ration. But where's he getting it from?'

'Edwards' farm' I gabbled. 'But we never ate a chicken from there. Never.'

'It wasn't a chicken he had in your tap room, it was steak. Beef. But how would he get it from Edwards' farm? Mr Edwards and young George have never been caught selling illegal meat.'

'I just thought,' my mouth went on, 'when I saw him at the Edwards' barn, he was up to no good.'

Constable Latham stretched a hand forward and gripped me by the shoulder. I was sure he was going to arrest me. The

handcuffs would be next. 'Good lass,' he said. 'There are dozens of people in this village happy to let the spivs get away with their evil crimes. I am so pleased a young citizen like you is on the side of the law. We need more people like you. Ready to risk their lives to catch the villains.'

'Our lives?' I gibbered.

'Oh, yes. The business is called the black market. They make huge amounts of money by breaking the ration laws. So those cheats will do anything to stay in their filthy game. They would even kill people who inform on them.'

'Inform?'

He nodded. 'People like you,' he said.

Chapter 5

Turnips and truncheons

Constable Latham kept his hand on my shoulder as he marched me down the road to the White Horse Inn.

'We're not open yet, Mr Latham,' Dad said. 'You should know that. If I served you a drink at four o'clock you'd have to arrest yourself. Hah! Hah!'

The special constable didn't laugh. 'I have come to ask if I can borrow your daughter,' he said. 'She is a witness to what could be a very serious crime.'

For a moment there was panic in Dad's eyes. He was thinking the same as I was. Chicken dinner. Chicken pie. Black Market. Prison.

'Serious crime?' Dad squeaked.

'I have reason to believe there is a black market operating from a nearby farm. Your daughter has seen a suspicious character in the vicinity and I need her as a witness,' Constable Latham said slowly.

Dad scratched his chin. 'Have you got any homework to do, Rosie?'

'No, Dad.'

'Then I suppose you'd better go with the constable. If you're going to be running round farmyards you'd better change into your old skirt and your boots. If you get your school shoes dirty your mum will kill me.'

'Yes, Dad,' I said and ran upstairs to change. When I returned to the tap room the policeman was supping a glass of Golden Ale. Dad passed me a torch. 'You'll be needing this,' he said. There was a shield across the glass that let out a small spot of light. 'It's dark out there now. Mind you don't bump into any pig bins.'

'I know where they are, Dad,' I told him. Everyone put their waste food in the bins on street corners and the scraps were used to feed pigs. When they were fat enough they killed the pigs and ate them. The truth is you could smell the bins long before you reached them. Rotting turnips and cabbage and mashed potato and carrot and apples and dried egg and bread. I was glad I wasn't a pig, having to eat that stuff.

I stepped out into the blacked-out street. There were low clouds in the sky so there wasn't even starlight to guide us down the empty streets. Blackout curtains were drawn tight but the streets still gave off a sort of glow. The enemy bombers would find us if they wanted to, Mum said.

I led the way out of the village and onto the road that led to Edwards' Farm. The policeman's giraffe neck seemed to peer round corners before we reached them. His voice was piping like the recorders we played in school.

Suddenly I knew why. Special Police Constable Latham was scared.

Then something else made sense. He didn't need *me* to show him the way to Edwards' Farm. He wanted me there because he was afraid to go alone. I remembered what he had said the night before about the black market rogues: 'They will do anything to stay in their filthy game. They would even kill people.'

'Have you got a gun, Constable?' I asked.

'I have my truncheon,' he said.

'That's good,' I said. Maybe he could use his truncheon to bat away the bullets when the black market dealers shot at us.

There were lots of bombing raids on Portsmouth. The enemy bombers wanted to sink the warships in the harbour. The same warships Mum worked on. Every time the sirens went we hurried to a shelter and waited for a bomb to drop on our heads.

So I was used to it; I was used to spending hours waiting to die. I wasn't afraid of bombs. Now I wasn't afraid of bullets. I took a deep breath and said bravely, 'We'll be all right, Constable.'

But I wasn't so brave about meeting a ghost.

Chapter 6
Winds and Wells

The wind rustled the ragged bushes at the entrance to the yard of Edwards' Farm. The gate led to a path with the farmhouse on the left and a large barn on the right.

Everything was in darkness, as I expected. If there was anyone in the farmhouse they would be snug behind blackout curtains. They could still hear us if we made too much noise. Farmers have shotguns. I could picture Farmer Edwards rushing to the door and blasting at us.

The latch on the
gate creaked as Constable
Latham tugged at it. The
hinges creaked a little too as we
stepped through the gateway. We stood
perfectly still, waiting to see if anyone
had heard.

'All clear,' the special constable
whispered. He turned to close the gate
behind us but a gust of wind caught it and
flung it shut against the gatepost with a
crash that would have woken the dead in
Portsmouth graveyard.

I sighed. A dog barked in some distant kennel. The dry branches of the bushes rattled against the gate. No farmer with a shotgun. 'So far so good,' the policeman said.

I pointed towards the barn. He vanished round the far end of that building,' I said.

The giraffe neck shot out as if Mr Latham expected to see Slick Sam peeking back. 'When I say "go" I want you to run to the corner and check that it's all clear,' he said.

'Why don't you go?' I asked.

'I'm a big target. And I'd be noisier than you. Better if you go. Wave a handkerchief if it's safe and I'll join you.'

I took a breath and ran on my toes. I trod in soft, squishy stuff that I hoped was mud—though I knew from

the smell that it wasn't. I looked carefully around the corner. The wall of the barn was blank as Miss Wearmouth's blackboard after I'd cleaned it... and I got to clean it a lot as a punishment for talking in class.

I waved my handkerchief and Mr Latham loped across the yard towards me. He groaned. 'What's wrong?' I hissed.

'I think I put my foot in something nasty,' he whined.

'Where now?' I asked.

'Hush!' he said.

'What?'

'Listen.'

I listened. I heard men's voices. They were chatting and laughing. There were other odd noises too but I couldn't work out what they were.

'We've found the butcher shop where they cut up the secret supplies of meat,' he said.

'How do you know?'

'The noises,' he said. 'That is sawing of bones, and that is a meat cleaver chopping up joints. I should be a detective, you know.'

He was right. I had heard the sounds in the butcher shop on Drayton Lane.

'They're inside the barn,' I said.

Special Constable Latham was panting a little. In the faint light I saw him raise his truncheon and creep carefully along the front wall of the barn until he came to a door. There was no light showing. The wooden walls were cracked and twisted so they must have been well covered with blackout curtains.

'You go first,' the policeman told me.

I lifted the latch, opened the door and stepped forward.

The inside of the barn was dark as the bottom of a well at midnight. The place was empty.

Chapter 7
Torches and traps

I pushed the switch on my torch and shone it around. There were bits of farm machines and piles of hay, scythes and wagons and horse harness and cart-wheels. There were ropes and rags and sacks and bags, spider-webs and dust and grease and cracked buckets. But no butchers.

Mr Latham stretched his neck to look over my shoulder. 'I can still hear them,' he croaked. Sure enough the sounds of men talking and laughing was still drifting on the calm barn air. That's when I suddenly thought of ghosts. It was a phantom farm. We were hearing the spirits of the long-dead farm hands.

I froze. I wanted to turn and run all the way home like the little piggy in the rhyme. But my feet seemed stuck to the floor. Miss Wearmouth told us ghost stories. I never

knew if they were true. Now I was sure they must be... and I was in the middle of a ghost story.

Mr Latham broke the spell. 'They must be in a building at the back of the barn,' he said.

I blew out my cheeks and breathed again. 'Of course. That must be it.'

We slipped out of the barn and back into the yard. We were tiptoeing to the back of the barn but I wasn't sure why. Another deep breath and I looked around the corner. There was a haystack. It was the shape of a house and almost as large as the barn.

I waved for the policeman to follow me. We shone our torches on the stack. We could still hear the sound of men's voices but there was no one there. Just a haystack.

A haunted haystack. I think my heart stopped beating for ten seconds.

The constable and I walked around the hay and back to the barn. We circled them twice. The voices never stopped and yet we couldn't see who was making the sounds.

Then we heard the rattle of a diesel engine as an old lorry chugged down the lane. It stopped at the gate. We heard the same sounds we'd been making ten minutes before as the farmyard gate opened, then closed. We watched from the shadow of the corner of the barn. The lorry headlamps glowed through the slits in black covers. Enough light to see the path; not enough light to show us hiding.

The lorry pulled round to the back of the barn and parked next to the haystack. The driver tooted three times on his horn turned off the engine, opened his cab and jumped down—a man as tall as Constable Latham but twice as heavy.

'They will do anything to stay in their filthy game. They will even kill people,' I muttered. I hadn't believed it before. But this man looked the sort who would snuff us out like a candle. I stayed frozen and silent and watched something amazing.

I saw a ray of light shine from the corner of the haystack. It grew wider. It seemed

as if the haystack was opening up... and
it was. The stack
was a wooden hut,
covered in hay to
disguise it.

Not a haunted haystack on a phantom farm after all.

As the door opened wider I saw Farmer Edwards and his son George smile a greeting in the light of the oil lamps for the lorry driver. He closed the door behind him.

'There's a plough at the side of the barn,' Constable Latham said. 'We can jam it up against the door and trap them inside. We can get the Portsmouth police to arrest the lot of them red-handed. They'll go to prison for twenty years!'

There was a soft click behind us. A voice said, 'I don't think so.'

We turned slowly. The soft click was a knife blade opening. The voice was the man holding the wicked weapon. He'd stayed in the cab when the lorry driver went inside the haystack. He'd crept down and caught us. We thought we were crime hunters—we'd just been hunted.

The man with the knife was Slick Sam.

Chapter 8
Cows and carves

Sam forced us to walk into the butchery inside the haystack. The smell of blood made me feel sick. Bits of meat dripped onto the straw on the floor. Worst of all, the faces of the Edwards family and the driver were full of fire and fury. Their red-stained hands held glittering butchers' knives.

'Constable Latham, isn't it?' the farmer said. He was short and powerful with black hair turning grey at the sides. His hot-cheeked son had muscles like a strong man in a circus.

'I am arresting you on suspicion of evading the ration laws of this country,' the constable said boldly but his voice was shaking.

'I don't think so,' Slick Sam said again. 'You think you are helping the people win this war? You're not. It's people like me and Mr Edwards that's doing that, Mr Copper. People are hungry and we're feeding them.'

Everybody wants a little bit extra, I remembered my dad saying.

'It's against the law,' the policeman whined.

'There's no law against killing an old cow and selling the meat,' Slick Sam sneered. 'There's just a law against getting *caught* doing it.'

'And I caught you,' Mr Latham said.

Sam tested the blade of his knife against his thumb. It looked sharper than Dad's razor. Mind you, a rusty sheet from a tin roof was sharper than Dad's old razor. Thinking of Dad brought a tear to my eye. I knew I wouldn't see him again. Not a bomb, not a bullet. A knife would finish me off.

'My dad knows where we are,' I said. 'He said if we weren't home by seven he'd call the Portsmouth police.'

The black market men looked at one another. Farmer Edwards spoke at last. 'It's no use, Sam. We're finished.'

Sam snarled, 'We can carve up the copper and sell him as best steak. Nobody needs to know.'

Young George Edwards spoke for the first time. 'But we can't hurt a girl, Sam, we can't.'

'I can,' the spiv argued. 'Leave her to me.'

The lorry driver stepped forward, moving like one of the battleships in the harbour. He grabbed the spiv's wrist and twisted till the man in yellow shoes cried out and dropped the knife. 'No,' he said. 'We're thieves, not killers.'

He looked at Special Constable Latham. 'Nobody likes you, Latham. Even the real

police look the other way when we hand them a nice piece of steak or a couple of pound notes.' He nodded towards the strips of meat hanging from a rail. 'This was just a cow that died of old age. The law says we should report it to the ration people. Every farmer knows that. But any farmer will just sell it to hungry families. You don't *have* to arrest us.'

The Constable stretched his

Nat Jackley neck as far as it would go. 'I do,' he said. 'And I am.'

I'd been so sure I wanted to see the villains behind bars. But I thought of the chicken I'd eaten. I was no better than Slick Sam. And I thought of the hungry families.

Everybody gets the same rations so we share it out, fair and square, Dad had said. *But it's not that simple,* he'd added.

***

The next day we finished our maths lesson early so Miss Wearmouth said, 'We have time for a story. I think today I'll tell you a ghost story.'

'There's no such things as ghosts,' I said.

Her eyes were like swollen gooseberries behind her little glasses. 'Don't be cheeky, Rose. If I say there are ghosts there are ghosts.'

'But...'

'But nothing. You can miss your break time and clean my blackboards.'

'Yes Miss Wearmouth,' I said with a sigh. And she told us a tale about a haunted barn.

That break time I cleaned the board with a smile on my face. Haunted barns? No such thing.

Epilogue

The butcher shop hidden inside a haystack was a clever idea. The special constable tracked them down by following the man who tried to sell the meat in the town— the 'spiv'.

The farmers were caught cutting up meat. They said it was an old, dead cow— not stolen—but they were arrested, fined and sent to prison.

There were dozens of ration rules and thousands of people broke those rules. Most of them got away with it because the police couldn't lock away half the country... the police pretended it wasn't happening.

The laws in wartime sometimes gave the wrong people the punishments. A woman fed her own scraps of bread to the birds in her garden and was fined twelve shillings.

A shopkeeper was fined five pounds for selling sweets he made from his own sugar ration.

Yet some lorry drivers got away with some really big frauds. If one of them had a lorry full of food he might park in a quiet spot. He would go for a walk while a couple of crates were stolen from the back. The thieves would leave the driver a packet of money and sell the food for a fortune. The wealthy people could afford the stolen food, the poorer hungry families stayed hungry while the thieves got rich. They usually got away with it.

The little criminals were punished; the big criminals escaped.

What would you have done if you'd known a farmer selling his dead cow?